AF409702

ISBN: 979-8-9943237-3-1
Hardcover | Ultra Premium Color

Published by Grace & Grit Books
United States
First Edition
Printed in the United States of America

To the beautiful imaginations that make the world beautiful.

It was Thursday.
Thursdays were for projects.
Thursdays were for planning.
Thursdays were for building something brilliant.
Jean Harper sat beside Juju.
She smiled when Juju's curls started to lift.

Juju had an idea.
A very bright, buzzy idea.
BZZZT!
Then another.
Then three more.

Her brain spark-spark-sparked.
Markers popped open.
Paper shuffled.
Glitter tilted dangerously close to the edge of the desk.
Her curls lifted higher.

HISTORY
HISTORY
SCIENCE

She leaned close to her project.
She whispered a word she had just built.
"Zapple..."

SCIENCE
HISTORY
SCIENCE

"...Flapple."
Bzzzzzzzz.
The air shimmered.
Her pencil trembled.
BUZZ.
A streak of yellow zipped into shape.

STARRE
HISTORY
SCIENCE

The Zapple-Flapple crackled onto her desk.
It had lightning-shaped wings.
It hummed softly, like sunshine in a jar.
"Add glitter!" it fizzed.

HISTORY
SCIENCE

Juju grabbed the glitter.
"More tape!" it buzzed.
She reached for the tape.
"Make it spin!" it zipped.
Scissors.
Glue.
Sparkles.

SCIENCE
HISTORY
SCIENCE

Her one project became two.
Two became three.
"Wheels wobbled."
"Towers tumbled."
"Paint splattered into a dizzy swirl of color."
Juju's hands moved faster and faster.

STORY
GEOGRAPHY
HISTORY
SCIENCE

Every time Juju switched ideas,
Bzzzt!
A tiny yellow spark flickered into the air.
Bzzzt!
Another spark.
Soon little zig-zags shimmered around her desk
like happy fireflies.

STORY
GEOGRAPHY
HISTORY
SCIENCE

Jean tilted her head.
"I can't see it," she said softly.
"But I feel sparkly."
Across the room Mr. Alder paused mid-step.
For just a second he thought he saw a thin streak
of yellow light dart across the classroom wall.
He blinked.
Nothing.

GEOGRAPHY
HISTORY
SCIENCE

Juju looked down at her desk.
Four beginnings.
Not one ending.
Glitter here.
Tape there.
Half-spinning wheels wobbling gently.
"Oh."
Her curls slowly settled.

She took a breath.
"Glow Slow," Juju whispered.
The tiny sparks hovered.
Not gone.
Just waiting.

12 13 14 15 16 17

"Glow Slow."
The sparks drifted closer.
Closer.
Until one warm golden glow shimmered above her desk.

It floated down.
It rested beside her project.
Not buzzing.
Not zapping.
Just shining.

11 12 13 14 15 16 17

Juju picked one idea.
Just one.
She found a small sturdy box.
She painted it the color of midnight.
Inside she built a tiny world of golden wires
 and foil.
Carefully she guided the Zapple-Flapple's
glow into the center.
She closed the lid.
Carefully.
Brightly.
Completely.

0 11 12 13 14 15 16 17

Juju closed her eyes.
The sparks inside her head were still buzzing.
Jean Harper smiled.
"Ideas don't have to race," she said softly.
Glow Slow. Jean said, "You did something again!?"
Juju grinned.
"We made it shine."
Juju tapped the lid of the midnight box.
"Glow Slow," she said softly.
And inside the corner of the box,
almost too small to notice,
a faint yellow flicker.

ABOUT THE AUTHOR

Dr. JeVona Maniex is an author, Human Resources Consultant, Industrial Organizational Psychologist, and creator of stories that celebrate imagination, friendship, and the power of words.

She believes language is one of the greatest tools children have to build worlds, solve problems, and discover who they are becoming.

When she is not writing, she is dreaming up new adventures for Juju July and encouraging young readers to play boldly with their own words.

ABOUT THE SERIES

The Juju July series follows a creative girl whose imagination has
a way of turning words into something much bigger than expected.

Each book explores how language, friendship, and courage shape
 the world around us.

www.ingramcontent.com/pod-product-compliance
Lightning Source LLC
Chambersburg PA
CBRC090747110726
48005CB00008B/989